The Jesus Tree

To D. J. and Robbie Dellinger
May you always remember the joy
of Christmas at Grandma Dellinger's house

The Jesus Tree

Annetta E. Dellinger
Art by Susan Stoehr Morris

Laurie and Elizabeth woke up feeling excited. They had big smiles on their faces.

"Today's the big day!" they yelled as they hopped out of bed and quickly got dressed.

Mother and Daddy had big smiles, too. They were just as excited as the girls. Elizabeth and Laurie ate their breakfast and then wiggled into their warm coats.

"Let's go," said Daddy. And they all walked out to the car.

The girls whispered and giggled as they looked out the car window. "How much longer?" asked Laurie. "I can't wait!"

"Here it is," Daddy replied as he pulled the car into the evergreen tree farm.

Laurie and Elizabeth jumped out of the car. They skipped up one row of trees and down another. They saw tall trees, short trees, fat trees, and skinny trees.

"This one feels soft," said Elizabeth.

"Ouch!" cried Laurie. "This one is sticky!"

"Sh-h, come peek in here," whispered Mother. "There is a little bird nest hidden in the branches."

"Look at this tree," Daddy said. Mother felt the long, soft needles. The children smelled the fresh pine smell.

"Yes, we want this one! It smells just like a Christmas tree!" the girls laughed.

Cutting down the Christmas tree was fun. But the girls were still excited. Tonight something else would happen.

Just before bedtime, Elizabeth and Laurie snuggled in their mommy and daddy's arms by the Christmas tree. They liked to feel the warm fire and listen to the pine cones on the tree crack open.

They liked to talk about the birthday cake they would make for Jesus.

"I like to blow out the candle and lick the icing," said Elizabeth.

"I like to sing happy birthday to Jesus REAL LOUD!" shouted Laurie.

"But I know something that is even more fun," Daddy added with a silly grin on his face. "It's eating the cake!" Everyone laughed.

"PLEASE, PLEASE, tell us about the decorations. I can't wait any longer," Laurie begged.

Mother winked at Daddy. Then she began to tell the girls about the decorations on the tree.

"The Christmas tree is called an evergreen tree. It always stays green, even in winter," said Mother. "That reminds us that Jesus is alive and that one day we will get to live with Him in heaven for ever and ever."

Daddy put lights on the tree. Then he turned out all the lamps in the room. "O-o-o! It's dark!" Laurie squealed, reaching for Mother's hand.

Then Daddy plugged in the cord, and the bright Christmas tree lights flashed on and off, on and off.

Daddy said, "When it's dark we can't see where we want to go. We feel afraid. Jesus says when we are afraid we can talk to Him. He will take care of us. Jesus is our Light and He shows us the way to heaven."

Laurie squeezed under the tree to help Daddy pull the soft, white cotton around the tree trunk.

"It looks just like a big pile of snowflakes," she laughed.

"You're right, Laurie," Daddy laughed. "God makes every snowflake different. And God makes people different, too, because each person is very special to Him."

"There's nobody in the world just like you, Elizabeth," Mother said as she kissed her on the nose.

"How about ME?" interrupted Laurie.

As Daddy leaned over to give her a big hug, he smiled and said, "You are one of a kind. There is no one in the world like you either."

"Yippee!" shouted Laurie.

"It's my turn to help," Elizabeth said as she hung the angel on the tree.

As she did, Daddy told the girls about the angel who told Mary she was going to have a baby. The angel told her to name the baby Jesus.

Then Daddy told Laurie and Elizabeth about the angel who visited the shepherds in the fields. The angel told the shepherds where they could find the newborn baby wrapped in cloths and lying in a manger.

"The multitude! The multitude!" Laurie interrupted. "My Sunday school teacher told me that big word. It means LOTS and LOTS and LOTS! There was a *multitude* of angels who filled the sky and sang praises to God."

"And don't forget about the angels that watch over us every day," added Elizabeth.

Mother hung a soft woolly lamb on the tree. Beside it she hung a candy cane. "The candy cane looks like the stick the shepherds used in the fields as they took care of their sheep. The Bible tells us that Jesus is our Good Shepherd and that we are His little lambs. He takes good care of us."

Each of the girls hung a bell on the tree.

"Bells make beautiful sounds," said Daddy. "People make happy sounds when they sing songs to Jesus."

"The round ball ornaments can remind us of the beautiful world God created," Mother said.

"And we can tell everyone in the whole wide world about Jesus," Laurie happily added.

As mother stepped back to look at the tree, she said in a soft voice, "All the different colors on the tree make it beautiful. And God made His world beautiful, too, by creating people with different colors of skin."

Elizabeth handed Daddy a big, shiny star. Daddy reached high on tiptoe and put the star on top of the tree. Then he told Elizabeth and Laurie about the Wise Men.

"Long ago some wise men who studied the stars noticed a special new star in the nighttime sky. They traveled to the big city of Jerusalem where King Herod lived. They asked King Herod if he knew where they could find the newborn King."

"King Herod told them to go to Bethlehem," said Daddy. "The Bible tells us the Wise Men followed the bright star in the east until it stopped over the place where they found the Baby Jesus. Then they gave presents to Him."

Just then Laurie ran to her room shouting, "I'll be right back!"

Mother and Daddy and Elizabeth all looked at each other in surprise as they listened to Laurie run up, and then back down, the stairs.

"Close your eyes, REAL TIGHT!" she commanded. Then she quietly put three little presents under the tree.

"Open your eyes now," Laurie continued as she hopped onto her daddy's lap. "I made presents for you because I love you. I made them all by myself!"

"Thank you," they all said as they clapped for Laurie.

"That's what Christmas is all about," Mother said. "God gave us the very first Christmas gift, His Son, Jesus. That was God's way of showing us His love," Mother reminded them.

The children snuggled close to their mother and daddy. "I like our Christmas tree. It's beautiful," whispered Laurie.

Elizabeth whispered something in Laurie's ear. Laurie got so excited that she had a big, happy smile on her face.

"Yes, yes, let's!" Laurie whispered.

The girls grabbed hands and jumped up in front of the Christmas tree. Then together they said, "Everything on our Christmas tree reminds us of Jesus. We think we should call it our Jesus Tree!"